SHOUT FREEDOM!

by

Rick Otley and Tray Brown

DORRANCE
PUBLISHING CO
EST. 1920
PITTSBURGH, PENNSYLVANIA 15238

Dorrance Publishing Co
585 Alpha Drive
Suite 103
Pittsburgh, PA 15238
Visit our website at *www.dorrancebookstore.com*

ISBN: 978-1-6453-0674-0
eISBN: 978-1-6453-0664-1

Cast of Characters

Moses Brown   Slave, husband to Annie May, father to Martha, John, and Isaac

Annie May Brown   Slave, wife of Moses, mother to Martha, John, and Isaac

Martha Brown   Slave, daughter to the Browns

John Brown   Slave, son to the Browns

Redd   Plantation owner, husband to Mary, father to Richard and Luke

Mary Redd   Wife to Redd, mother to Richard and Luke

Richard Redd   Aspiring plantation owner, son of Redd and Mary

Luke Redd   College gentleman, son of Redd and Mary

Hiram Lynch   Slaveowner

Rabbit   Slave

William Floyd   Reverend of the First Episcopal Church of Galveston

General Granger   Union Commander of the Department of Texas

Soldier   An aide to General Granger

The following character may appear on stage or their voices may be heard offstage

Auctioneer

Voice 1

Voice 2

Slave 1

Slave 2

Various church voices and freed slave voices

This story takes place in Galveston, Texas, during the spring and summer of 1865.

The setting is the corn plantation of Master Thomas Redd. He owns two dozen slaves who live in two separate quarters from the Redd estate.

It is April 16th, Easter Sunday. Confederate General Robert E. Lee has surrendered the last major Confederate army to the Union's Ulysses S. Grant at Appomattox Courthouse five days before. Most in Texas have not heard the news; however, Master Redd and other affluent men are aware. But life goes on as usual. At the moment Master Redd is angry with his slaves, who are behind in planting corn.

Act 1, Scene 1 – *The slave quarters of Moses Brown, a middle-aged slave who, although in fine physical shape, his countenance is often one of resignation. He and his family belong to Master Redd, who bought the Browns from his Master Redd's brother, Big Redd, three years ago. The Brown family consists of Moses; his wife, Annie May, a vibrant, optimistic woman; their teenaged son, John; and teenaged daughter, Martha. Martha is lighter skinned than her parents and brother. Because of her light complexion, Master Redd has her work in his house, assisting with everyday chores and cooking. Her brother and parents work the cornfields. The Browns have just returned from a slave church and are getting ready to observe the Easter Sunday. They enter with excitement.*

Moses: Now you children git yer selves to helping yer mama fix dinner. I'm gonna look at dem chickens out back and see if any eggs came out.

John: She got dinner going just fine. Why we got to work on Sunday, Pa? I thought dis day was a day of rest.

Moses: Help your mother, hear me?

(Moses leaves to check the chicken coop.)

Annie May: There is no day of rest for the mother. Now get over here and help with deez butter beans or I'll make you cook deez goat livers.

Martha: Livers? Again?

John: Well, I know we got the shrimp. Deys always shrimp in Gavelstone.

Martha: Galveston, Texas.

John: Mama, I hope you know I just joking. I love me my shrimp! But I like chicken, too. We ain't gettin' no chicken fo' Easter?

Annie May: Yes, we have a chicken today. Master Redd gave us dem chickens to do what we want with 'em.

Moses: *(offstage, from outside)* Come back here, you devil.

Annie May: I s'pect yo' father is getting one ready for us now.

Martha: You mean—he's gonna kill one.

Annie May: *(laughs)* Well, yes, child. They gotta be killed first. But we only got eight grown chickens and dey need ta last until a few of the chicks grow. 'Sides, when we eat a chicken, it's less eggs for us days ahead.

John: I'm gonna go watch him break that chicken's neck! *(heads for door)*

Annie May: You ain't going nowhere. Get them beans ready.

John: *(dejected)* I hate lima beans. *(He heads over to his mother to help.)*

Annie May: (*smiles*) Deez "butter beans."

John: And we ain't got no butter.

Annie May: Didn't you ask Master Redd for some butter yesterday when you was workin' in da house?

Martha: He was in such a angry mood yesterday, I didn't say nothing to him. I jest polished furniture and cleaned curtains all day.

John: You lucky he ain't got you in there working today. You know he always has his brother's family visit fer holidays.

Martha: I didn't ask if he needed help...and he didn't say nothing.

Moses: (*entering with a dead chicken*) Master Redd is coming and he ain't looking Christian today.

Martha: I wonder if I should hide?

John: Where you gonna hide in here?

Redd: (*from outside*) Brown! Moses Brown! (*comes to door and lets himself in*)

Moses: Master Redd, do come in. Happy Easter.

Redd: I gotta tell you people something. My Easter ain't happy and I ain't either. We are way behind on the plant schedule and yesterday you slaves didn't do nothing.

Moses: I thought we got much done yesterday.

Redd: Don't talk back to me, nigger. You are lucky I ain't got you out there right now.

John: Well, if you hadn't of sold my brother, we'd have more help to be helping.

Moses: Young John, be still with your tongue.

John: I miss him, Father. He was my brother. I miss him bad. He taught me good how to do things and he was my friend. Ain't dat many young slaves to be friends with because everybody always workin'. And da one friend I had, he gone. It's been more than two Easters ago that my brother be gone. Broke his leg pass fixin' because of dem horses. And by summer he was always with his crutch. And then he was solt again. Like we was to you. He was a good brother.

Moses: And he still is. He's just not here with us.

Annie May: Solt to some man going to San Antonio. My heart cried a lake of tears that day.

Redd: That day was a good day for your son. He doesn't have to work in the fields like you slaves do. And from what I hear, he's the best farrier there is down there. Maybe someday he'll be a blacksmith, if he's lucky.

Moses: I miss my son. Isaac was a good boy.

Redd: He got a bad leg, Brown. I can't keep a cripple here and have him do nothing. And I ain't got a need for someone to shoe horses. You're lucky I sold him to another Christian man who appreciates his niggers.

Martha: I hear San Antonio is hot as hell.

Annie May: Martha!

Redd: I didn't come to talk about your son and my business decisions. I came over here to tell you that we need to be up earlier than usual tomorrow, because we are a week off schedule. We should have thinned out them carrots yesterday.

Moses: We will git to it early tomorrow, Master Redd.

Redd: You better! Or I'll put the whip to all you. *(looks at Martha)* And I need you out there working, too. Until all my carrots are done.

Redd: And the other slaves look up to you, Brown. So, it's on you. Get them other slaves to work extra hard...or I'll be extra hard on you. With my whip! (*He leaves.*)

Act 1, Scene 2: *Dinner table at the Redd Plantation house. Redd is surrounded by his family—his wife, Mary, a woman who has come to terms with compromise. She accepts being the wife of a slave owner; sons, Richard Redd, early twenties, known as "Lil' Redd," and Luke, who is a couple of years younger than his brother. Luke is home from the university and he has a different ideology about slaves than the rest of his family.*

Redd: (*finishing a prayer*) ...and we ask for thy continued love and endless bounty. Amen. Now let's take a look at that ham. Lovely.

Mary: Thank you, Mister Redd. It's wonderful to have such a nice meal with my whole family here with me.

Redd: (*to Luke*) Yes, son. Your mother has missed you fiercely.

Mary: And you father has, too.

Luke: Well, thank you both. I'm grateful for such a nice dinner, Mother.

Redd: She made it all herself. No help from the girl.

Luke: You mean Martha? You gave her the day off to be with her parents on Easter? Well now, Pa, you are getting to be a soft touch, ain't ya?

Redd: I wouldn't go that far. Your mamma just wanted to do something special for her boy. It's not easy when your child just up and leaves and goes off to fancy Baylor University.

Richard: How you liking Independence? I hear that they got the tallest oak trees anywhere in Texas.

Luke: I like it a lot. The whole town is a busy place and with Baylor being there—

Redd: (*cuts him off without thinking about it*) That's where General Sam Houston used to live.

Richard: President Sam Houston Mary. And now he's gone.

Richard: (*a slave owner in training*) Looks good, Mama. Did you cuss out them niggers, Pa?

Redd: I told them they had better worker harder and faster or I'm taking a whip to all of them. (*laughs*)

Richard: Let me do it, please, Pa! I need to learn how to do it right.

Redd: We will see, Lil' Red. We will see.

Luke: Seems strange to be talking about whipping slaves. It being Sunday and all.

Mary: Now, Luke, your father knows best. Slaves work better under pressure.

Luke: No one works better under pressure, Mother. Do you?

Redd: Now, boy, don't go smart talking to your mother.

Richard: Or else, you may get the whip, too.

Redd and Richard enjoy the joke.

Lights crossfade to the Browns, who are eating at the table.

Martha: This chicken tastes ugly, Mama.

Annie May: Ain't the chicken. It's these old forks. Tastes like lead.

Martha: Master Redd's got nice forks. All silver and polished up fine. I ought to know.

John: (*eating with his fingers*) Steal us some, girl. I don't like eating with my fingers.

Moses: (*with a chuckle*) Oh, yes. That's right. This boy's a fine gen-tell-man. He wants that silver fork.

Annie May: Now husband, there ain't nothing wrong with a good fork.

John: Master Redd won't give us no good forks or knives. (*starts to snicker*) He's 'fraid we gonna sneak out in da night and kill him with 'em.

Moses: Very amusing. We havings forks...and he having rifles.

John: Member when Ol' Franklin ran off last Christmas. Ol' Redd chased after him—but Franklin got gone before Ol' Redd found out.

Annie May: But Redd had a horse and a pistol and Franklin was just an old, bare-foot, slave on his way to God knows where. I think when he turnt fifty he said he had had enough.

Moses: But they never found that nigga. He was crazy. But he got away.

Annie May: I hope dat so.

Martha: I never heard no braggin' about him bein' catched. I think he gotta away.

John: To where? New Orleans? Ain't no place for a slave.

Moses: Unless he be looking to be sold.

Annie May: May God Bless him.

Moses: God Bless him.

Lights crossfade to the Redds, who have finished dinner.

Mary: (*clearing the table*) Here I am, having to clean up this mess from you boys. All by myself.

Redd: (*sitting in a comfortable chair, more like a throne*) We enjoyed the meal, Mother.

Luke: It was really good, Mama. I knew you could cook a nice dinner if you tried.

Mary: It wasn't about the trying, it was more about the wanting. (*proudly*) I'm not used to having to cook for my three hungry men.

Redd: I had to give the girl a day to be with her family.

Luke: Bad enough she had to work last Christmas serving us all. And Papa's friends, too.

Mary: Martha having the day with her family is just fine with me. I think I'm just spoiled from having her over here doing things.

Luke: Doing *everything*, you mean.

Redd: Luke, what's making your mouth so sassy today?

Richard: (*enjoying an after-dinner smoke and doing nothing*) I think he's in love. (*laughs*)

Redd: The boy's too young to be feeling love. (*laughs as well*)

Richard: (*watches to make sure his mother doesn't see him crudely grab his crotch*) Wouldn't know what to do with it, if he found it. (*more laughter*)

Luke: (*who has been helping his mother clear the table*) Very amusing.

Richard: I'm not trying to "amuse" you, little brother. I seen the way you were staring at Martha yesterday when she was reaching up and cleaning the chandeliers.

Luke: I was not. I don't know what you are talking about.

Redd: He had better not be looking over a slave girl. She may be lighter than most of them, but she's still one of them. Just not so black—like the others. (*using his unique logic and proud of his analysis*) Hell, even a dog has different color pups in a litter.

Mary: (*unfazed by the analogy*) Now, Redd, people ain't dogs, husband.

There is a knock at the door. Mary goes to answer it and welcomes fellow slaveholder Hiram Lynch, who appears excited.

Redd: Well, Hiram, (*shaking hands*) what brings you over to our little piece of heaven on an Easter Sunday?

Lynch: Redd, I need to speak with you privately.

(The other family members hear this and leave the room.)

Redd: What is wrong?

Lynch: I just got word from a couple of dockworkers that Lincoln was killed.

Redd: What!?

Lynch: Shot by some actor. Honest. During a play performance. On Good Friday!

Redd: You better not be teasing me, Lynch.

Lynch: Oh, hell no. The murder of their president don't bother me the none, I'm won't lie about that.

Redd: Hmm...perhaps this is a good thing. Perhaps that Emancipation Lincoln made up will go away now.

Lynch: That ain't likely. It's law now and has been the law. 'Course you ain't breakin' the law if nobody know you are breakin' it, right?

Redd: Ha...we gotta have some hope, eh?

Redd: Yes.... This means that Johnson is President. The traitor. He ain't a Yankee, but sure knows how to act like one.

Lynch: Who knows what to make of a man when you don't really don't know where he stands.

Redd: You still ain't told your slaves about that Emancipation, right?

Lynch: No. Never. They gonna have to find out on their own. (*He laughs.*)

Redd: And they can't read. (*He laughs.*) And they ain't talking to strangers. Best to keep them ignorant or else we are going have to pay 'em....

Lynch: I don't see me doing it anytime soon. We just keep our niggers busy and always remind them how lucky they are to have us.

(Lights crossfade to Moses and Annie Mae, who are sitting outside of their shack. Both are in their rocking chairs and looking up at the sky. It is night.)

Annie May: When are we ever going to be free? We've been slaves ever since we was children.

Moses: Well, woman. Tears ain't gonna change anything.

Annie May: I've been praying. I've been praying every day and night. Seems like the Lord just ain't list'ning.

Moses: (*tries to comfort her*) Well, I know you ain't gonna give up. We are people. People of color. There will be a change. Someday. There has to be.

Annie May: I just don't know. It doesn't seem—

Moses: And you gonna give up? Just like that?

Annie May: I don't know how much I can stand. It ain't right for a woman my age to be plantin'...and picking corn and cotton. I'm getting old. I would like to be comfortable. Not working all the time. Not being someone's property to do and please as the master wants. This ain't no life. What about our children?...What about us?

Moses: What about us?

Annie May: What about *all* of us?

Moses: (*frustrated*) What about us? The Lord has heard our prayers. And the Lord has provided. What more can we do?

Annie May: (*weeping*) I'm not supposed to be an animal. Just existing. I am a person. One of God's children. I am a woman. A woman who can't take much more...and I want to see hope for our children. Will it ever end? Will us slaves ever be free?

Moses: Woman. Peace. Peace, be still. Lights fade out.

Act 1, Scene 3: *Back at the Redds'. A puppy is being born.*

Mary: Come on, little one. You can make it. Mama, c'mon.

Richard: Spill those babies, bitch.

Luke: That's ugly talk to a mother-to-be. You can't talk to Sandy like that.

Richard: She can't help she is a dog.

Mary: She gotta deliver.

Richard: Here they come, Mama.

Luke: Oh, my Lord. Look at that. (*observing the puppies being delivered*) Beautiful, huh?

They admire the newborn pups.

Crossfade to Master Redd, at a slave auction. His eye is on a slave named Cye.

Auctioneer: This one is starting at two hundred. A steal. Come on, gentlemen, who's the first to bid on this buck?

Redd: Two hundred.

Voice 1:   Two ten.

Redd: Two twenty.

Voice 1:   Two thurty.

Voice 2:   Two fifty.

Voice 1:   Two forty.

Redd: Two fifty.

Voice 1:   Two sixty.

Voice 2:   Two seventy.

Voice 1:   Two eighty.

Redd: Damn it to hell. Three fifty.

Silence

Auctioneer: Sold! Three fifty. Slave 9A Lot B. New Orleans' Christ of Angels Thomas Hunter Cargo Company. A Flatlander Kanga from Senegambia.

Cheers go up!

Voice 1:   Look at those legs.

Voice 2:   Those hamstrings are meant for cotton-pickin'.

Auctioneer: Or breeding! Next up is a nigger that will serve you forever. Meet Hiram. He's an experienced nigger at cotton, sugar, beans, corn, and every other crop.

Redd walks over to slave 9A.

Redd: What's your name, nigger? You speak English?

Rabbit: (*an angry young man who has had enough of slavery*) Rabbit.

Redd: Hell of a name. Hopefully, you'll breed like one. I'm glad you can talk.

Rabbit: And be you who?

Redd: Your owner. Now we going to Galveston, boy. Yer new home.

Act 1, Scene 4: *Inside the parlor of the Redd home. Martha is dusting the elegant furniture. She looks over at the piano from time to time. After a pause, she walks to the doorway to make sure no one is watching. She goes to the piano and begins to play a pleasant tune. She is careful not to play too loud. Her talent of playing piano without lessons is her secret.*

Luke appears in the doorway, unseen by Martha as she plays. She finishes her song and begins to weep. Luke is moved by her display of talent and emotion. He leaves as to not embarrass her, but not before a second look.

Act 1, Scene 5: *Master Redd is in his study sitting at a fine desk, where he unlocks a drawer and withdraws an old newspaper. Trying to read the faded ink he speaks aloud, as if trying once again to comprehend the implications.*

Redd:	(*reading aloud*) "And by virtue of the power, and for the purpose aforesaid, I do order and declare that all persons held as slaves within said designated States, and parts of States, are, and henceforward shall be free; and that the Executive government of the United States, including the military and naval authorities thereof, will recognize and maintain the freedom of said persons." Nonsense! They can't just take away a man's property! That's not American. Hell, I don't have to obey any President except President Jefferson Davis. And Andrew Johnson sure as hell ain't my president. He ain't taking my workers away from me. I bought them slaves. (*Silence. He thinks to himself for a moment.*) How in the Hell are them niggers ever going to be free? They can't survive without my generosity. Some people are meant to be slaves. People of color have been in bondage ever since the biblical days. Now they want to be free. Thinking they gonna get married, raise families, live in houses like white people? Someday owning their own businesses! I ain't telling them nothing, no way. Oh, I can see them now, getting down on their knees and whining for help. "Jesus, oh Lord, help me, me Jesus. Lord, help me, Jesus, Lord, help me, God. Ha, ha, ha, ha, ha. (*He is mocking his slaves and laughing.*) Lord, help me, Jesus! (*He regains control of himself.*) They are only gonna be free from me when they die.

Act 1, Scene 6: *The Browns are in the First Episcopal Church of Galveston. The congregation is black and so is the minister, Reverend William Floyd. The absence of white men at a black church is rare but does occur.*

Rev. Floyd: I need you to listen to what Joshua said. In chapter 6, we learn that bondages are our walls. The people of Israel had crossed the Jordan River into the land of Canaan. The land of milk and honey that God had promised them. Now on the eastern banks of the Jordan was the city of Jericho. The city of Jericho was no friend to these new immigrants. Families were being torn apart and homes being torn down. Finally enough was enough. Joshua went to God and he was told to march. March around the city walls. Marched around it for six days. On the seventh day, they got up at daybreak and did as Father in Heaven told them. They were to march around and circle the city seven times. The seventh time around they shouted. And they shouted. They yelled out, "Shout freedom!"... "Shout freedom!" We need to yell out "Shout freedom!"

(Congregation yells, "Shout freedom!")

Rev. Floyd: Our bondages, our barriers will fall down. We must just "Shout freedom." I tell you, one day, my sisters and my brothers, there will be freedom for all people. Freedom for all people! Amen!

Act 1, Scene 7: *Outside of the Redds' plantation house. Master Redd has his whip out and the newest slave, Rabbit, is tied up to a tree. Richard is there as well, watching.*

Redd: I can't believe you were gonna try to run off the plantation like that. Ain't you know that we always find our slaves.

Richard: I knew I'd find him, Pa. Can't no slave outrun a horse.

Redd: Looks like you beat him up pretty good. I guess he didn't want to come back.

Richard: Not until I tied him up. He didn't have a choice after that. He knows I was gonna shoot him if he didn't let me take him back.

Redd: I'd rather cope with a dead slave than a runaway. (*to Rabbit*) Are you stupid, boy?

Rabbit: I's sorry, Master Redd. I juss too tired from pickin' corn and can't do no more. My back be hurtin' and my fingers be filled with dem blisters. I's in no condition to work. I just needed some time for my body to—

Redd: From now on you are gonna live closer to me. In the Negro Brown house. Them slaves are well behaved. Maybe it'll rub off on you. Anyway, where the hell were you going to go? (*chuckles*) You people get brave and try your escaping from your owners, but you got no idea where the hell you are where you going to go and what you are going to eat, and how you gonna sleep. Plain stupid.

Rabbit: I can barely stand up.

Redd: And you won't at all stand up at all when I am done with ya. (*drawing whip up to strike*)

Rabbit: Yes, Master. I'm sorry. I'm gonna be a better slave. Just don't whip me, please.

Redd: Then let me hear you beg.

Rabbit: Please, Master, please, Master, don't whip this poor, broken, stupid man. Please, please, Master Redd. I beg of you.

Redd: (*laughs*) Stop your whining. It ain't manly. (*Redd begins whipping Rabbit as the lights fade out.*)

※

Act 1, Scene 8: *The kitchen inside the Redd Plantation house. Martha is drying dishes. Luke is reading poetry to her.*

Luke: "*Mine eye and heart are at a mortal war,*
How to divide the conquest of thy sight;
Mine eye my heart thy picture's sight would bar,
My heart mine eye the freedom of that right."

Martha: (*cleaning, yet interested, no one else speaks to her intellectually*) I know what a heart and eye are at mortal war. All I have to do is look in one of your mother's mirrors.

Luke: It's Shakespeare. Very beautiful words saying deep ideas. (*continues to read*)

"My heart doth plead that thou in him dost lie,
A closet never pierced with crystal eyes,
But the defendant doth that plea deny,
And says in him thy fair appearance lies."

Martha: Sounds like Master Shakespeare wants to know truth.

Luke:　　　(*admiringly, smiling*) Who don't?

(*They laugh and Richard reads the next quatrain.*)

Richard:　　　*"To 'cide this title is impannelled*
A quest of thoughts, all tenants to the heart;
And by their verdict is determined
The clear eye's moiety, and the dear heart's part."

Luke:　　　I have no idea what "moiety" is. (*thinks*) But perhaps it means being apart.

Martha:　　　(*moves closer to see the poem*) That's a nice poem, but it ends with them being apart?

Luke:　　　No. There is this couplet. It goes like this. (*reading*)

"As thus: mine eye's due is thine outward part,
And my heart's right, thine inward love of heart."

Martha:　　　(*laughing*) I have no idea what a couplet is, except maybe it being about two. Sounds like he love her.

Luke:　　　I think so, too, Miss Martha.

Martha:　　　Miss Martha? Ha. I have never heard anyone call me "Miss Martha." (*She laughs.*) Oh, Mister Luke.

Luke:　　　Luke.

Martha:　　　Luke. (*intimately*) Luke...everyone calls me "girl," "nigger," "light nigger." But I am who I am. Strange looking or not?

Luke:　　　(*gazes at her, grabs her hand, and holds it*) You are perfect.

Lights fade.

Act 1, Scene 9: *Physically healed from the brutal beating, Rabbit looks out of his shack's door. He sees miles in front of him and he dreams of freedom.*

Rabbit: My father, my grandfather. What would dey had done? I can't live this life anymore. Lord. (*approaching tears*) I don't reckon I ever known no freedom. If I be good enough to have it, I could stand me that. But when? When? (*looks…thinks*) There is an ocean out there. Freedom is out there. It is out there! Not here in Texas! Not in no New Orleans. Ain't no freedom anywhere for this man.... (*thinks more*) All I got to do is swim. Yes, like Moses parting that sea. I swim for my freedom. (*drops to knees*) Oh, Jesus. Help me swim. Help me swim to freedom. I don't know where it is. But I want to be there. I need to be there with freedom. Show me, Jesus. Show me where freedom is.

Act 1, Scene 10: *The next morning, Martha is in the Redds' kitchen cleaning off silver utensils.*

Luke: (*walking in*) Cleaning the forks and knives you can't use. My father is wrong in his ideas. I apologize.

Martha: Welcome back to the house, Mister Luke. And there no need to be ashamed. It's what I do.

Luke: And your ma and pa, brother, you and Rabbit are eating with your hands? (*ashamed*) My father is a thoughtless man.

Martha: We have some old forks that Missus Redd was throwing away.... Sometimes we use twigs to make forks. My father (*don't tell your father*) can make a knife out of any piece of wood. He's much smarter than he let's on.

(She laughs. He does, too.)

Luke: Good for him. (*looking at the silverware*) This ain't knives and we use. My parents have an abundance of forks. (*contemplates and then*) Here, take these to your mama and papa. You people need to use them. We don't.

Martha: Are you certain, Mister Luke?

Luke: "Luke." No more "Mister" Luke. Yes. Yes. I know what is right.

※

Act 1, Scene 11: *It is dinner at the Browns' shack. They are at the table using the new forks and knives. Moses is showing John how to cut a chicken apart. Rabbit is lying on the floor in pain.*

Moses: Right der son, right in dat place der.

John: I see it.

Moses: You got it. Mother Brown! We ready with this chicken.

Annie May: Looks so good. And smells so good.

Moses: Oh, yes. We smoked it good. Mesquite. I heard someone call it. (*thinks*) We have more chickens than las' month. (*looks over at Rabbit*) Not up to eating, Rabbit?

Rabbit: Maybe later.

Annie May: Poor man is still trying to heal from that beating. And still has to work.

They sit the table, Moses prays.

Moses: Holy God, we thank you for this chicken we are going to—

There is a knock at the door. Master Redd lets himself in. He is drunk.

Redd: I'm visiting all my slaves tonight. I want to make sure we all know it ain't smart to have ideas about leaving. You ain't free. No slaves are free. And all you really got is me. (*Redd looks at the table.*) And my knives and forks. (*angry*) What are you niggers doing with my knives and forks? Tell me! Where did you get them? (*pause. No one answers.*) Well? ...Who gave them to you? It wasn't me! Wasn't my wife. Wasn't my boy, Richard. (*He looks them all in the eye and then goes berserk, tossing the chicken and other food on the floor.*) You people ain't eating nothing. I tell you what—it better not been Luke. Was it? Was it?!

No one answers. Master Redd goes to the empty table and picks up the silverware. The Browns sit quietly. Redd takes the items and storms out but slips on the way out, falling on his back. He is slow to comprehend that he is on his back. Moses gets up and walks over to him. He offers his hand to Redd to help him up.

Brown: Master Redd. Let me help you.

Redd: (*very proud, pushing Brown's hand away*) The hell with that. (*slowly gets up...grabbing the utensils*) I don't need no help.

(Redd slowly stands up and walks off back to his house as Brown goes back to his chair. After sitting down he looks around at his family and they burst into laughter.)

End of Act I.

///

Act 2, Scene 1: *It is late May. The East Texas coastal heat is evident in the clothing and countenance in all of Galveston's residents. At Master Redd's plantation, his slaves are busy harvesting corn. Master Redd and son Richard are watching over them.*

Redd: Now don't be picking any of that corn that doesn't have dark silk. You got that, John Brown! We'll come out here next week and get the rest of them. There's plenty of perfect corn to be picked and that will keep everybody busy for all the week. I just can't believe it came so quick to harvest this year.

Richard: (*counting the kernels on an ear*) Eight hundred kernels on this one, Pa. And this one is mighty average.

Redd: Those stalks are seven-footers. And most of 'em got two ears. We should do good on this harvest.

Richard: (*yells at Rabbit*) Make sure you look for that second ear on every stalk, Rabbit! I know how lazy you are getting in this Texas sun. A lot hotter, I bet, than that sun in New Orleans, or wherever you are from.

Redd: Damn. They work slower every day. It's going to be a coffin nail to get them to work hard come July.

Richard: It's hard for people to want to work hard when they are working for free.

Redd: What would they need payment for? I give them a way of life they couldn't have on their own. They have their place to live and I feed them well. And we both know they are better with me than without me. Or else—

Richard: Or else what, Pa? You'd free them? Are you trying to convince me that you ain't giving these slaves freedom is because they are better off with you than being free? Because, I might tend to agree. But we both know this ain't got nothing to do with that.

Redd: I don't believe that was what I was going to say. But if I pay them, they will have to pay for their own room and board. So, it would come out about even, I figure.

Richard: Well, I guess they won't know until someone tells them they are free.

Redd: What are you saying?

Richard: Come on, Pa. I know all about the Emancipation papers that Lincoln signed before he got killed. The slaves are free. Nothing has changed. Johnson ain't changing it. Foster won't change it.

Redd: They will know soon enough.

Richard: And when they find out? How will *they* drink that elixir?

Redd: They'll be happy enough to be free. They won't be thinking none about me, son. They're gonna find out how expensive that damn freedom is when they get it. People got to eat. Free or not.

Richard: You know they know about the surrender in April. They know about Lincoln. They even know about those two blockade runners that the town folk went insane over. Old women running in the streets with pieces of, uh, whatever it was called.

Redd: The "Lark." Just happened. Last Wednesday. Biggest thing happened since the King of France come visit. And I would bet, everyone knows about that.... These slaves talk. We know they do. And they are talking hopeful talk. After all, there is no more blockade. The Union prevailed and Confederates have lost this horrible war and paid with their blood. Things will be changing swiftly.

Richard: And you? Are you ready for that change?

Cross-fade to the slaves working at removing corn from stalks.

Moses: The corn smells sweeter this year than last one. But I believe this be also another field.

Richard: Redd says he has twenty thousand plants on this one acre alone.

Annie May: And he has ten more acres waiting after this one.

Moses: The bastard.

Annie May: Now, Moses. Please don't let the devil in you today.

Rabbit: He's right! Redd is a bastard. He sells dis here corn for cows to eat. You know that? You dumb slaves know that, right? We eat turnips and cabbage and *sometimes* he lets us eat *our own* corn. But this corn is cattle corn. Not even for people.

Moses: But we always got shrimp!

Annie May: Well, the cows got to eat, too.

Rabbit: (*mocks her*) "The cows gotta eat"…Jesus!

Moses: Now Rabbit—

Rabbit: When does this end? I want to be free! I want to run away from all of this. (*His voice grows louder.*) I am a slave to NO man! And I pity the man who sets me free!

Lights up on Redd and Richard.

Redd: What are you hollerin' about, you jackass?

Silence for a moment. The slaves exchange looks.

Rabbit: I'm thirsty.

Act 2, Scene 2: *Sunday - The First Episcopal Church of Galveston*

Rev. Floyd: In the book of Matthew 12 it says in the 39th verse:

"For as Jonas was three days and three nights in the whale's belly; so shall the Son of man be three days and three nights in the heart of the earth." My people, here is Christ referring to a man who would not fulfill his mission, and now he is inside of the belly of a great fish. Many people believe the story of Jonah and the whale to be just a fish story...and not based in fact. But I know—we know—what it is to be swallowed up in the belly of a whale. *To be swallowed up in the belly of captivity....* And what does Jonah do? He endures. Yes, he endures, and then he gets spit out onto land by the monster fish and he goes to Ninevah. He goes to complete his calling and to turn the hearts of the sinful, prideful peoples of Ninevah to change their evil nature. And so shall we. Soon we will be free. Our time in the belly of the whale will end. But, perhaps, the whale is a symbol of many things that keep up in darkness. People—beware of the whales. Beware of those other people, those habits, those things that keep you in the belly of darkness. Because there is light. And we must endure. We must keep a-trying. We must.

Act 2, Scene 3: *Monday, May 29th. Rabbit is outside of his cabin. He is speaking to himself. He is tired. It's the end of the day.*

Rabbit: Mannde mo jogii freedom. When? When this freedom? I smell the air. The salt. The sea is so close and I can swim like a fish. And even if I don't make it—I has for me a great big whale waiting for me. That whale will take me home. Take me home to freedom. That whale would. He be my freedom whale.

John has been listening in and approaches.

John: I like that. That Freedom Whale.

Rabbit: That might be the only whale we are gonna be seeing, if we get our any freedom.

John: I never known no freedom. You were free once?

Rabbit: In my country. When I was the age of you. My own peoples tied me up and sold me. Erupted my life. And that was jest the first time. I've been sold many times.

John: Why is that? You can't find a home?

Rabbit: Home? Hell, boy. When you a slave you never at home. I just been with many masters. They all the same. Bullies. Want everything. Give nothing. Take everything.

John: They take what?

Rabbit: My freedom, you ignorant boy. The master will take whatever you let him take.

John: Master Redd is better than his brother, Big Redd.

Rabbit: Oh?

John: We lived with his brother for most my life, but Master Big Redd make a deal to get us over here for some other slaves that Redd traded him for us. It all happened fast. We are with one brother one day, and we at Redds' the next.

Rabbit: The whole family?

John: And my brother, Isaac. All us. Been a few years, it seems. Redd makes us field workers and takes my sister indoors to be a house servant. And sells my brother away.

Rabbit: Lucky for her. Probably for him, too.

John: And what about you? You got a story?

Rabbit: I wanna think I got me a story. But it ain't good. My story is looking for freedom. I search so hard that I jes wanna shout, "Freedom! Freedom, where is you?"

John: Life could be worse. Dem slaves in Arkansas got it real bad, I heard.

Rabbit: Slaves got it something awful everywhere. Ain't nothing to be proud of—being a Texas slave. Good God. None of us got a story if we let someone else write it. My story is that I am a slave. That ain't no story.

John: Maybe someday you be free and write your own story.

Rabbit: Maybe so…maybe so. I want my story to end with me bein' free.

Act 2, Scene 4: *After dinner in the kitchen of the plantation house. Luke and Mary are playing checkers.*

Luke: King me!

Mary: Son, you are so good at this. (*laughs*) Stop beating your mother so bad.

Luke: It's all mathematics, Mamma.

Mary: Well, look at that. You won again. (*She laughs more. She doesn't mind losing. She's just happy her son is home.*)

Luke: (*leaning back in his chair and basking in victory*) I'm the best there is at Baylor. No one has beaten me yet!

Mary: Goodness! And I never win. The only ones I can beat are your brother and our house girl, Martha.

Luke: You taught Martha checkers, huh? I think you had something to do with teaching her how to play piano, as well, huh? Ya know she knows how, right?

Mary: I know. And I don't mind it. But I suspect your father would. He doesn't think the slaves have any reason to play music, and probably shouldn't be foraying in to such. He doesn't even like them singing. He has always viewed his Negroes as slaves. Just slaves.

Luke: And Mother, those slaves shouldn't even be slaves.

Mary: What are you talking about?

Luke: Lincoln freed them! Everyone knows that. Everyone but the slaves.

Mary: Yes, I have heard rumor that they were—

Luke: Freed a couple years ago by Lincoln.

Mary: But that don't apply to Texas.

Luke: How can it not? We're a state. The Union doesn't recognize Texas succeeding. It's not as if we are our own country down here.

Mary: Well, there are more Confederacy soldiers here, that I've seen, than Union.

Luke: Not for long. The Union has control of the harbor.

Mary: It's only temporary.

Luke: Are you jesting? The Union is here to stay. Soon there will be more of them. And they will free the slaves. And then what?

Mary: I have no idea. The slaves need us people to watch over them and take care of them. How will they exist without your father keeping them busy?

Luke: "Keeping them busy!" Momma, listen to yourself. It's not for one man to keep another man busy. Daddy ain't doing them any favors by keeping them "busy."

Mary: I'm just saying that they are productive now. I don't know that they will be so when they are freedmen and women.

Luke: Soon we will find out, and what do you think they are gonna do when learn that you people have been hiding the truth from them? Do you think they will say, "That's just fine, Mrs. Redd. No hard feelings"?

Mary: I—

Luke: They won't! And if you don't tell them soon, I might.

Mary: Please don't. There is no telling what your father would do if he found that you are causing contention. That is for your daddy to do. I mean, he will eventually tell them. He will have to, son. Especially if another nearby plantation owner tells his slaves the truth.

Luke: The "truth"? …I like that. So when the word breaks free—then the slaves are?

Mary: Seems reasonable.

Luke: And you think father is gonna lead that charge? Ha! He won't tell the servants anything.

Mary: He will. When it is the right time. Your father knows what is best for his slaves.

Luke: "Our" slaves... "Your" slaves. They are yours also...Mother.

Act 2, Scene 5: *The Browns' slave quarters. The Browns are asleep. Rabbit is sitting on his bed. As he listens to Moses snoring, he takes a gulp out of a bottle. After a few moments, he staggers to stand up and makes his way out the door. A bit away from the house, he talks to himself.*

Rabbit: I can't be sleepin' with dat snorin' ev'ry night. (*He looks around.*) Redd and his group are sleepin', or so it seems. I ought to git in there right now and kill that devil. Yes, I should. I got this bottle from Master Redd's shed. Easy enough to steal. I bet I could steal me a knife jes as easy. 'Course, getting caught horrible. Redd might jes kill me. I know'd he would beat me something terrible. (*He takes the last sip of the bottle and throws it. He takes a moment to enjoy his apparent drunkenness and then starts to become frightened and starts searching for the bottle.*) Master Devil Redd will hurt me if he see dat bottle out here. Where is you, bottle? Oh, there you is. Right under my nose. My bottle, my friend.

John has awakened and walks outside and joins Rabbit, who continues saying, "My bottle, my friend."

John: Oh, my, what have you done done, Rabbit? Where'd you get that? It ain't Christmas.

Rabbit: You watching me? Why you hiding and watching? I can't trust nobody.

John: No, man. No. I heard you out here. You getting kinda loud. But now, seeing that bottle, I think that something bad could come from it.

Rabbit: Ain't much good come from whiskey, boy.

John: Seriously, Rabbit. Whatcha gonna do when Ol' Redd find out his bottle is missing?

Rabbit: I thought I might put some water in here and then put it back. Be like he never know. I wanted to be free.

John: You gonna be free to scream when you are tied up to a tree getting whipped.

Rabbit: I don't think I thought this out. I was jes so anxious to get drunk.

John: And look it where got ya.

Rabbit: (*suddenly aware of his situation*) I think I better go.

John: Go back to bed and face the truth in the morning.

Rabbit: I mean, I'm going to find freedom. I'm going to make myself free right now.

John: No, you ain't. Now get back to the house before you get us all in trouble.

Rabbit: No!

John: (*goes to grab him to take him back*) Come on. You're drunk. And you ain't free.

Rabbit: But I is.

The two struggle for a moment until Rabbit raises the bottle as to strike John. When John sees this, he lets go of Rabbit.

Rabbit: (*looks at the plantation house*) Goodbye, Redd Devil.

He then runs off. John watches for a few seconds in disbelief and then follows after him.

※

Act 2, Scene 6: *Outside of the slave quarters. It is morning of the next day. There is a frenzy to find Rabbit and John as Redd, Richard, Luke, Moses, Annie May, and Martha search for Rabbit and John.*

Annie May: Son? Son, answer me! Where are you?

Redd: He snuck off with that uppity slave, didn't he? (*shouts*) You two better show yourselves now!

Martha: John would never run off. He just would not do that, Mama.

Redd: Slaves do anything to get free.

Moses: My son ain't stupid.

Redd: But that Rabbit is!

Richard: And I'm gonna whup 'em both when we get them, huh, Pa?

Redd: Gotta find 'em first. Get the horses.

Annie May: (*falling to ground, praying*) Please, dear Lord, help us find my boy, help us find them both.

Redd: (*falls to ground, and mocks her*) "Please, dear Lord, bring back my slaves to me. Help my sons find them." (*stands up*) God will listen to *me*, woman.

Annie May: Shame on you, Master Redd.

Mary: (*who is just now arriving onto the scene*) What is the fuss about? Redd, who is missing?

Redd: Two of our slaves, Mary. And we need them. We have much work ahead of us today.

Mary: Maybe they are on a stroll before they have to get out in this hot Texas sun.

Annie May: (*looking off in distance*): Who is that? Is that my son? Son!

John enters, distraught. Goes to his mother as the others gather around them.

John: I'm here, Mama. I'm fine.

Redd: Good. Where is that damn Rabbit bastard?

John: (*addressing his mother*) He's gone, Mama. The fool ran to the beach and—

Redd: Jumped on a boat? Ain't no one escaping Galveston with the Union here now.

John: Mama, he ran to the ocean, I chased him, but he was too fast. It was like he had lightning in him. He get to the water and runs into the water and all the while he is yelling——screaming—"Here, I am, freedom whale. Here I am. Save me. I am going home"... He started swimming and I was yelling at him to come back and he keep yellin' back to me that he was gonna swim back to his home. He say that God would give him a whale to get back home on.

Annie May: Son, oh, my son.

Redd: Did you help him escape?

John: No, sir. I stayed there a while, looking for a whale, and sometime later Rabbit come back on the sand, dead.

Redd: Then he is ready to be buried. Stupid man! Go get his body, Richard! Take a big horse and a rope.

Richard: Yes, Father! (*He exits excitedly.*)

Redd: (*to John*) You sure you didn't plan on escaping with him? Were you part of this?

John: No, sir.

Redd: I'm going to be keeping my eyes on you, boy.

Mary walks to Redd and tries to comfort him.

Mary: It will be fine, Mr. Redd. We will get the crop in. I will go out there and help.

Redd loves her, hugs her. He appreciates her blithe spirit. Martha walks over to Luke. Moses and Annie May hold each other as well.

Moses: Thank God our boy is alive.

Annie May: Thanks be to God, Moses Brown.

Martha: (*She has made her way to Luke and it is now apparent that they are close. She puts her head against him and sobs, he comforts her.*) I thought I'd never see my brother again, Luke.

Luke: He's here. And innocent.

Martha: Thank Jesus.

End of Act 2.

Act 3, Scene 1: *June 18ᵗʰ, 1865. Sunday morning inside the Redd Plantation home. Union General Gordon Granger will soon arrive at Galveston Island with 2,000 federal troops. Redd and Lynch are inside the Redd home, drinking coffee.*

Lynch: I heard Joe Clark, over in Goat Island, say that the Union's boys and a general are coming into Galveston soon to tell the slaves the truth.

Redd: General Granger. You heard of him. Chikamauga. The lookout place, I hear it tell. Couple of years ago…around Gettysburg time. You don't want to be on the wrong side of a lookout point, huh? Georgia did *not* do their duty!

Lynch: That's in the past, Redd. Now they got a chip on their shouder. They comin' here soon to tell our slaves they are free. Then what? I got crops that gotta be tended to, and I spent lots of money on those nig—

Redd: (*cutting him off*) I think we ain't got a boat to float with here, Lynch.

Lynch: I was thinkin' we get our servants together and head west. We can start over. We got money. I got money…ain't you, Redd? You got money, too. Government don't care about the West.

Redd: (*thinking*) I don't know. Seems with a harvest coming in we need workers. And them Mexicans don't work as hard as the black.

Lynch: They all work hard when you holding a whip. Now, you coming with me? …If not, I might be interested in coming to an agreement for the value of my property, providing you have the means? Redd…hmm? I have plenty of carrot and cauliflower coming in any day.

Redd: I think we can agree on something, Lynch.

Lynch:	(*thinks and with a chuckle*) My wife would never let me. Some people are meant to be forever in Texas.
Redd:	And I can't blame them.
Lynch:	Is your brother staying? Does Big Redd know the inevitable is coming?
Redd:	I haven't talked to him in a few weeks, but he usually knows when something is in the air.

Mary enters, carrying some vegetables. She goes to the kitchen area.

Mary:	Are you two gentlemen figuring out how to fix the problems in the world?
Lynch:	Well, somebody has to, Sarah Redd.
Mary:	Well, please let me know what you to decide. I don't want to be the last to know.
Redd:	Mary, why are you carrying those? We have a girl to help with that. Where is Martha?
Mary:	Master Redd, now you know it's Sunday, don't you? She probably is at that church they go to.
Redd:	Oh, yeah. Ain't that something. Ya know, Lynch, I made my slaves get baptized and then they go and start their own church.
Lynch:	Man, you don't really want them in yours, do ya?
Mary:	Maybe we should go to church today. We still have time to get ready.
Redd:	No thanks.
Lynch:	Redd, you ain't been to church in over a year, and that was for a funeral.

Redd: I don't like church much. Seem I go to feel better about life and I walk out of there feeling like a hypocrite. So I just don't go. I know who I am and I know Jesus loves me or I wouldn't be so blessed with a beautiful wife, my sons, my friends, this land, and my slaves. Yes, yes, indeed, I have been blessed by God, but there's no reason to go to church and feel guilty about it.

Lynch: Makes sense.

Mary: Well, a person should feel guilty when they go to church or else what is the reason to go? We all have sins.

Redd: Well, you are a woman, and more inclined to be spiritual. Now in a man, that can be a weakness.

Lynch: So true.

Mary: I'm need to wash these vegetables before I leave. Maybe they will be feeling spiritual tonight when we eat them, since you two can't. And don't smoke inside our parlor, please.

The men laugh as lights dim.

Act 3, Scene 2: *Martha and Luke are playing a card game.*

Luke: Thirty-one! That's a knock. I win!

Martha: Again! You always win.

Luke: Ha, ha! I can't help being so good. I will let you win one, however. But there's a price.

Martha: And what would that be for a girl with no money?

Luke: I was thinking maybe you could come up with some kind of prize.

Martha: Now, what would that be, Luke?

Luke: Well, use your imagination.

Martha: You want me to kiss you, do you? Why?

Luke: No, I just want you to win a game.

Martha: Sometimes I think you have love for me.

Luke: I think I do, too.

Martha: Maybe if things were different. Like me not being a slave in your house. Perhaps, if I was free, things could be different with us.

Luke: You will be free someday. And when that happens I'm taking you with me to Independence.

Martha: Really? Why?

Luke: I…I…like having you around.

Martha: Gonna make me *your* house girl?

Luke: More than that, sweet Martha. (*He gets closer to her, starts to kiss her cheek, and she turns her head after a moment to allow their lips to meet. They kiss.*)

(*As they kiss, Redd walks into the room and is startled to see the two kissing.*)

Redd: What the Hell are you doing, you idiot! Get away from her. (*He pulls Luke away from Martha and pins him against the chair or a wall.*)

Luke: Nothing.

Redd: Nothing!

Luke: Nothing wrong!

Redd: (*yelling and very angry*) You are not to ever touch her again. You understand!

Luke: Why?

Redd: Because she's a slave.

Luke: I love her!

Redd: She ain't like you!

Luke: I don't care!

Redd: She's a—

Luke: What?! What, Father? What kind of foul word will come out next?

Redd: She is your cousin, you stupid, stupid boy!

Luke: Meaning what?

Redd: Your uncle…he…is…a weak man when it comes to—

Luke: You mean he raped Annie May? Is that the story?

Redd: I'll show you…. (*He raises his fists to strike but stops himself as he realizes he is almost out of control.*)

Luke: Nothing. (*Luke walks past his father, who stares at the ground. As Luke walks out he grabs Martah's hand and they leave.*)

///

Act 3, Scene 3: *Night. The deck of a steamer. Union Commander of the Department of Texas, Major General Gordon Granger, looks out from the deck. He is balding, with a beard. A soldier approaches him.*

Soldier: Major General Granger, the captain says we will be in Galveston in a couple of hours.

Granger: Thank you, Major.

Soldier: Sir, the two thousand troops from Mobile and New Orleans are en route as well. They will arrive on the twentieth, as planned.

Granger: Galveston Harbor will be packed with steamers and soldiers before these people know what has hit them.

Soldier: Yes, sir.

Granger: I believe that two thousand Union soldiers in a town of seven thousand will make an impact. And the beauty of it is that most of the soldiers are Negro. Irony!

Soldier: Yes, sir. The Texans have not able to accept the surrender.

Granger: They will tomorrow. Tomorrow things are going to change in Texas!

Soldier: Yes, sir!

///

Act 3, Scene 4: *June 19th, 1865. Monday morning.*

Moses, Annie May, John, and other slaves are harvesting rice by hand. It is a new type of crop for Redd. The slaves, like most in Texas, are just becoming introduced to rice.

John: I don't think anyone gonna wanna eat this. Looks like weeds.

Annie May: Oh, people eat anything if they hungry enough. And if Master Redd don't like this, whatever it is, or can't sell it—we shall be eating it.

Moses: "Rice." They call it "rice." They is growing it in Lou-see-ana, so Redd think will grow here.

Slave 1: And what part of it do we's eat? Deez seeds?

Moses: That's the rice. You gotta cook it ta eat it. And we just doin' one part of this—harvesting this rice. After we fill up deez bags and we gotta take it all back to dat crop barn and den we gotta separate deez rice bits from the plant. Den we got take the green parts of de plants out to de south field and burn 'em.

Slave 2: I dunno if I can do dis all day. My back be killin' me all now.

Slave 1: Hell, man, you shouldn't be doin no complainin'. Old Annie May is a woman havin' to do this. While her daughter gets to work in the house.

Slave 2: She workin today inside again, Annie May? Maybe an older gal who knows more should be servin' the master inside.

Annie May: I ain't dat old, and Martha is inside doin' whatever they have her doing. It's Monday, so I'm thinkin' she washin' dishes and clothes.

John: Not together, I hope. (*pleased with his joke.*)

Slave 1: How can you be so happy? Havin; to do this is nothin' to be happy 'bout.

Moses: Now, it's all a matter of attitude. John got him a good attitude.

Slave 2: Moses, my back is killin' me.

Moses: Maybe you need to get your mind off it. We go lots more to do and we just getting started.

John: How about a song? Singing is good for a soul back. Mama, lead us in, uh, oh, let's try "Mercy Seat."

Annie May: Oh, yes, I love that one, too.

(Annie May begins singing the song. She sings for a few seconds and the others slowly join in.)

> "Oh, there is a calm, there's sure to be
> It's found underneath the mercy seat.
> Oh mercy seat, oh mercy seat
> It's underneath the mercy seat.
> There is a calm, oh, sure to be
> Around a calm on mercy seat.
> Oh mercy seat, oh mercy seat
> My peace is 'neath the mercy seat.
> "My peace is 'neath the mercy seat."

As they sing, Martha runs into the field with news.

Martha: *(excitedly)* Mother, Father, everyone. A negro soldier in a Union uniform came to the house and said we are to go to Ashton Villa on Broadway, now. He said to put down whatever we doing and come into town.

Moses: Whaaat? And Redd is alright with dat?

Martha: The soldier say we all got to be there. And now. He said that something needed to be read to all of us. Especially those that can't read.

Slave 2:   Well, Hell. Let's go! My back can't take it no more.

(They leave.)

Act 3, Scene 5: *Major General Gordon Granger is on the steps of a home. He is balding, with a beard. Surrounding him are soldiers, slaves and Caucasians. He surveys his audience and reads loudly:*

Granger: "The people of Texas are informed that, in accordance with a proclamation from the Executive of the United States, all slaves are free. This involves an absolute equality of personal rights and rights of property between former masters and slaves, and the connection heretofore existing between them becomes that between employer and hired labor. The freedmen are advised to remain quietly at their present homes and work for wages. They are informed that they will not be allowed to collect at military posts and that they will not be supported in idleness either there or elsewhere."

During Granger's reading there are shouts of praise and disbelief and when he finishes, there are exhibitions of jubilation and anger.

Gen. Granger: Now if you will excuse me. I need to tell every damn Texan I can find.

General Granger walks off. Slaves and Moses, Annie May, Martha, and John are embracing each other with joy. The Redds are stunned.

Annie May: Free! We are free!

Moses: Praise to our Jesus! FREE! I ain't never been free before, but I like it. And with all them soldiers with the general, I believe I'm gonna remain free!

John: I can't believe it! Now we can see Isaac!

Annie May: We can deliver him the news ourselves!

Martha: It's like a dream. I can't believe it!

Moses: Well. Best believe it! And the bad dreaming is over now. No more slavery!

John: No more slavery!

Lights dim on the Browns, who continue to discuss their future and come up on the Redds.

Richard: No more slavery? It ain't fair. I was gonna be a great slavemaster.

Luke: Well, now you are going to have to be a great employer.

(Richard angrily storms off.)

Redd: I knew this freedom was coming soon, but I wanted to get that rice in first. Damn! I don't like this! What about my rights? My right to own slaves?

Luke: To own other people?

Mary: I'm happy for them. Look at their joy! We will be fine, Redd.

Redd: Woman, are you stupid? Do you realize what this will do to me? To us?

Luke: Things will be different, for certain.

Lights up on the Browns, who cross over to the Redds.

Moses: Master Redd?

John: You don't have to call him "Master" no more.

Moses: "Mister" Redd. We thinkin' we will stay with you for a few days and then we will continue our freedom elsewheres.

Redd: And where you gonna continue this freedom you got now?

Moses: I think I might go up to that Independence that your Luke talks about. He says he going back soon. Maybe we go with him.

Redd: Are you crazy, man? You can't just go to some town and expect to get hired there.

Moses: I'll take my chances. My family don't want to be on no plantation for no more.

Redd: You people were born for the plantation.

Moses: And now we are reborn. Reborn with freedom!

Luke: I think Independence would be very happy to have you. Them people treat Negroes well. And there is always work. (*Luke takes Martha's hand.*) And I will help.

Annie May: It would be nice going to a place where black folk are wanted.

John: And the white people will be good to us.

Luke: I'll make sure of it.

Redd and Martha begin to leave.

Redd: We are going back to the house and figure out what to do about this. (*pause and then to Luke*) You coming, boy?

Luke: I think not. I will walk back with these…these free men and free women.

Annie May: Say that again!

Luke: Free men and free women!

Moses: And about time, too! I ain't getting any younger!

The Browns start to exit.

Annie May: Finally free. I want to shout it!

John: Do it! Shout freedom!

Annie May: Freedom!

John: Shout it again.

Annie May: (*laughing with joy*) Freedom!

John: Freedom!

Moses: Freedom!

Martha: Freedom!

Lights fade as the many shout, "Freedom!"

END